DRAGON JELLY

Claire Freedman

illustrated by Sue Hendra and Paul Linnet

BLOOMSBURY

NEW YORK LONDON NEW DELHI SYDNEY

Come to Max's MONSTER party.
There's GOO-LICIOUS food to eat!

It's creepy-crawly, stinky fun—
don't miss the SCARY treat!

First, it's monster pass-the-present,
which squiggles, shakes, and squirms,

and when the wrapping paper's off,
they find a nest of worms!

The hairy green magician
makes frog eggs disappear.

KAPOW! As if by magic,
frogs hop from Max's ear!

Hooray! It's bouncy castle time,
but this one's extra mucky.

As the monsters jump and bump,
it sprays out gunk—SPLAT-YUCKY!

The monsters need to cool right down.
Quick! To the blow-up pool.

It slops with buzzing botfly eggs,
and smelly fruit bat drool!

Next, it's the stinky breath contest.
Max wins without a doubt.

He turns the air thick yellow-green,
and all his friends pass out.

In messy monster hide-and-seek,
Max hides in a trash bin,

and as a great disguise, he wears
an old banana skin.

"Whoopee!" Max cries. "It's time to eat!
These termite tarts taste yummy.

Mmm! Glowworm wraps and earwig rolls,
and cockroach chips—so scrummy!"

Out comes the eyeball birthday cake
that SQUELCHES when you chew!

Max blows his earwax candles out,
then gobbles them down too!

"Monster food fight!" someone shouts.
The monsters duck and dodge.

The maggot cream goes flying,
and hits them all—SPLAT! SPLODGE!

TA-DA! It's DRAGON jelly time,
their scrumptious, sizzling treat.

It's red. It's wobbly. Best of all,
it's SCARY HOT to eat!

The bubbling jelly's gobbled down.
The monsters shake and hiss.

SWOOSH! Dragon jelly's so h-hot, smoke shoots out—just like this!

The monsters take home goody bags.
Yippee! Guess what they get.

A teeny, fiery DRAGON each—
the PERFECT monster pet!

For yuck-loving little monsters, everywhere! —CF

For Jake —SH

First published in Great Britain in September 2014 by Bloomsbury Publishing Plc
Published in the United States of America in July 2015 by Bloomsbury Children's Books
www.bloomsbury.com

Bloomsbury is a registered trademark of Bloomsbury Publishing Plc

For information about permission to reproduce selections from this book, write to
Permissions, Bloomsbury Children's Books, 1385 Broadway, New York, New York 10018
Bloomsbury books may be purchased for business or promotional use. For information on bulk
purchases please contact Macmillan Corporate and Premium Sales Department at
specialmarkets@macmillan.com

Library of Congress Cataloging-in-Publication Data
available upon request
ISBN 978-1-61963-682-8 (hardcover) • ISBN 978-1-61963-683-5 (e-book) • ISBN 978-1-61963-684-2 (e-PDF)

Art created with Adobe Photoshop
Typeset in Neucha
Book design by Zoe Waring

Printed in China by Leo Paper Products, Heshan, Guangdong
2 4 6 8 10 9 7 5 3 1

All papers used by Bloomsbury Publishing, Inc., are natural, recyclable products
made from wood grown in well-managed forests. The manufacturing processes
conform to the environmental regulations of the country of origin.